This book belongs to:

_____

This paperback edition first published in 2011 by Andersen Press Ltd.
First published in Great Britain in 1999 by Andersen Press Ltd.,
20 Vauxhall Bridge Road, London SW1V 2SA.
Text copyright © Jeanne Willis, 1999.
Illustrations copyright © Tony Ross, 1999.
The rights of Jeanne Willis and Tony Ross to be identified as the
author and illustrator of this work have been asserted by them
in accordance with the Copyright, Designs and Patents Act, 1988.
All rights reserved.
Colour separated in Switzerland by Photolitho AG, Zürich.
Printed and bound in Malaysia.

10   9   8   7

British Library Cataloguing in Publication Data available.

ISBN 978 1 84270 990 0

Susan Laughs

Jeanne Willis   Tony Ross

Andersen Press

Susan laughs,

Susan sings,

Susan flies,

Susan swings.

Susan's good, Susan's bad,

Susan's happy, Susan's sad.

Susan dances,

Susan rides,

Susan swims,

Susan hides.

Susan's shy,

Susan's loud,

Susan's angry,   Susan's proud.

Susan splashes,

Susan spins,

Susan waves,

Susan grins.

Susan's right,

Susan's wrong,

Susan's weak,

Susan's strong.

Susan trots,

Susan rows,

Susan paints,

Susan throws.

Susan feels, Susan fears,

Susan hugs, Susan hears.

That is Susan
through and through –
just like me, just like you.